The Pirate and the Potter Family

Set Sail For School!

Chapter | Page

Written by Michaela Morgan
Illustrated by Martin Chatterton

Chapter 1
Hide and Seek

One day they were playing Hide and Seek.

"Now it's your turn to find us," Lilly explained to Captain Kev. "We run and hide while you close your eyes and count out loud. Count one to ten."

The Potter family rushed off to find hiding places. Captain Kev closed his eyes and counted.

He found them immediately.
"You were too quick!" Billy shouted. "This time, count one to a hundred."
"Aye aye, mate!" said the pirate.
1, 2, 100!

That's when Dad realised there was a problem.

"Captain Kev," he said kindly, "you can't really count properly, can you?"

Captain Kev hung his head and blushed. "I never did be goin' to school," he admitted.

"Right!" said Gran. "We can soon sort that out. Come on, me hearties! Hoist the Jolly Roger and let's set sail for school!"

Chapter 2
Ready for School

Soon they were back at the Potter family's house getting ready for school. Captain Kev and his feathered friend were looking forward to their first day at school.

'Twill be a fine adventure!

Fine adventure!

Lilly and Billy were not so happy.

"We don't want to go back to school!" cried Billy.

"We want to go back to sea!" sobbed Lilly.

"Don't worry. We'll go back next school holidays," Mum promised. "For now, think about how surprised your friends will be when they meet Cap'n Kev and hear what you've been up to!"

But Lilly and Billy *were* worried. Mum didn't know about the Carter Crew, the bullies at school.

Chapter 3
Bullies!

On the first day of school, the Potter family trooped off down the street.

Dad, Mum and Gran went to the school office with Captain Kev. They needed to register him.

Lilly and Billy went into their classroom. The first kids they saw there were the Carter Crew.
"Oh no!" said Billy.
"Shiver me timbers!" Lilly agreed.
The Carter Crew got started straight away.
Look who's coming! It's Silly Billy …
… and his sister Lilly.
The Potty Potter Twins!

"Quiet now!" said the teacher.
"Now, who wants to tell us what they did in their holidays?"
"We sailed the seven seas with our pirate friend," Lilly piped up.

The Carter Crew sniggered.
"Liars!" they whispered.

That morning, the class had to paint a huge picture to go on the wall. All morning the Carter Crew picked on Lilly and Billy. When it was time to put away all the paper, paint and brushes, Colin Carter stuck out his foot. Billy went flying. The bullies laughed at him.

Billy blushed and the Carter Crew pointed. "He's gone bright pink!" they sneered. "Now he's going pinker!"

"And now here comes Lilly," giggled Colin. "Let's see if we can trip her up too."

But just then ...
Ahoy, classmates!
Captain Kev arrived!

He surprised Colin so much that ...

it was Colin that ended up going pink. All of the other children laughed at the bright pink bully.

Chapter 4
Class Act!

Every day, Captain Kev worked hard at school. First, he learned how to count from one to ten, and then from one to a hundred ... *properly!* The parrot helped as much as he could.

The Captain joined in with everything …

and he made lots of new friends. Even the Carter Crew became his friends. They gave up bullying and took up yo-ho-ho-ing instead.

The Captain helped the children (and the teacher) to learn new things too. He even taught them how to speak Pirate.

How to Speak Pirate

hello = **ahoy!**
yes = **aye**
yes, please = **aye aye**

very = **mighty**
scared = **afeard**
I am feeling very nervous! = **I be mighty afeard!**

Oh! = **Arrrrrrrrrrr!**
That's terrible! = **Arrrrrrrrrrr!**
That's wonderful! = **Arrrrrrrrrrr!**
What a good idea! = **Ooo-arrrrrrrrrrr!**

He was a star!

Chapter 5
What's Up, Cap'n?

But one morning Captain Kev woke up … and he looked sad. The Potters were worried about him.

"Are you missing the sea, dear?" Gran asked.

"Are you fed up with school?" Billy asked.

"Do you feel sick?" Mum asked.

"I be fine," said Captain Kev. But he didn't look fine.

Later that morning, Lilly heard a little noise. She looked up from her book to check on Captain Kev. The parrot was perched on the pirate's desk and was singing softly in his ear.

Captain Kev didn't see any of this. He kept his head down in his books and sometimes he sighed a small, sad sigh.

Then Gran arrived with a box. "This is for you!" she said.

Mum arrived with a banner.

Dad arrived with a present and the baby arrived with a card. (He had only taken a little tiny bite of it!)

Lilly and Billy and all the children came over with the things they had been secretly making.

"Ooo-arrrrrrrrrrrr!" said the Captain. He was so happy he just had to burst into song.